Halloween

Little Terry Tiddlemouse with brothers Snitch and Snatch

Together live quite happily in their house that's built of thatch.

Tomorrow will be Halloween, they'll all dress up as gnomes,

Then they'll call upon their friends and surprise them in their homes!

Terry wears a bright green suit and shoes with pointed toes,

His brothers wear bright red and blue with cherries on their nose.

They lift the latch at Mollie Mole's, she falls right back in fright,

She doesn't know her friends the mice, they all look such a sight.

Then Mollie gives them nuts to eat and dresses as a troll

And off they go the four of them to visit Cousin Vole.

His autumn windfall apples make a munchy meal,

Soon there's nothing left of them, no core, no skin, no peel.

Cousin Vole cannot decide what he's going to be,

A policeman or a postman or a tiny jumping flea.

But with pumpkin mask and cabbage tail, he goes as Mistress Mog,

The five of them then bounce along to visit Hector Hog.

Hector opens up the door to his house along the ditch,

It's no longer Hector Hog they see but a spiky hairy witch!

The six of them can only laugh as they look at one another,
Then all go out to one more house, the home of Hector's brother.

He bakes buns and tarts and cakes, his name is Roly-Poly,

He hums a tune if no one's there so he is never lonely.

They scoff the buns and drink his tea and then they all agree -

Buns are fun but best of all, the fun of Halloween!

Mollie Mole

Mollie Mole lives underground

In a cosy little house,

She has a good few neighbours,

Her favourite's Terry Mouse.

Her short thick coat is silky soft, the colour black as pitch,

Mollie does her digging in the earth along the ditch.

Mollie's snout is pink and bare, her claws are long and sharp,

She blunders in the daylight, she's nimble in the dark.

With digging done, a good night's work,

Her black coat washed and brushed

She's off to see her neighbours,

Especially Terry Mouse!

The Tea Party

Sir Cyril Squirrel met Mollie Mole and had a little chat

They took a stroll along the road to visit Robbie Rat.

He gave them tea and biscuits, jam tarts and strawberry cake,

They ate and ate and ate so much they all had tummy ache.

There came a knock at Robbie's door, it was his cousin Mouse.

She said, "I'll fetch the doctor and bring him to your house."

The doctor came and said "Aha!, you've all been very greedy,

I'm not at all the least surprised that you are feeling seedy!"

A dose of dreadful tasting stuff

Was given to each one

The doctor left a bottle full

And ate the last cream bun.

Sir Cyril Squirrel and Mollie Mole as well as Robbie Rat

On one thing all agree.

In future they'll not eat so much

When they sit down for tea.

Published by Ailsapress 2016
Port Charlotte Isle of Islay PA48 7TS
www. ailsapress.com

ISBN 978-0-9954912-0-5

Also by Joan Porter and Jessica Excell
'LITTLE TERRY TIDDLEMOUSE AND HIS COUNTRYSIDE FRIENDS'

Printed by Grafistar BV Netherlands
www. grafistar.nl